SERIOUSLY SCARY POEMS

Also compiled by John Foster

A Century of Children's Poems
101 Favourite Poems

Loopy Limericks
Ridiculous Rhymes
Dead Funny
Teasing Tongue-Twisters
Completely Crazy Poems

SERIOUSLY SCARY POEMS

Picked by John Foster

Illustrated by Nathan Reed

Collins

An imprint of HarperCollinsPublishers

First published in Great Britain by Collins 2003
Collins is an imprint of HarperCollins*Publishers* Ltd,
77-85 Fulham Palace Road, Hammersmith, W6 8JB

The HarperCollins website address is:
www.**fire**and**water**.com

135798642

This edition copyright © John Foster 2003
Illustrations by Nathan Reed 2003
The acknowledgements on page 95-96
constitute an extension of this copyright page.

0 00 714801 1

The authors, illustrator and editor assert the moral right to
be identified as the authors, illustrator and editor of this work.

Printed and bound in England by
Clays Ltd, St Ives plc

Contents

DOWN AT THE GRAVEYARD

MIDNIGHT PROWLERS

FRIGHTENING PHANTOMS AND GHASTLY GHOULS

CHILLING CREATURES AND PERILOUS PLACES

SINISTER SHADOWS AND NIGHTMARE SCREAMS

DOWN AT THE GRAVEYARD

Sinister Symphony

Warlocks whisper
Coffins creak
Tombstones tumble
Spirits speak

Phantoms frolic
Monsters moan
Serpents slither
Gremlins groan

Crones cackle
Demons dance
Am I staying?
Not a chance!

Paul Bright

Will You Come Down To The Graveyard?

Will you come down to the graveyard?
Will you come down to the graveyard?
Will you come down to the graveyard?

With me at twelve o'clock?

Will you walk among the gravestones?
Will you walk among the gravestones?
Will you walk among the gravestones?

And summon up the dead?

Will you whisper the Lord's Prayer
To keep you safe from harm?
Will you stand still in the moonlight
While the trees all sway and creak?

Will you come down to the graveyard?
Will you come down to the graveyard?
Will you come down to the graveyard?

With me at twelve o'clock?

Ian Bland

The Dance

Down at the graveyard at Hallowe'en
the earth begins to stir,
fingers appear, then hands and legs,
then mouths gasping for air.
The soil heaves
as bodies emerge,
pale from years under the ground,
as white as maggots,
almost translucent,
they hardly make a sound.
They spit the dirt from out of their mouths,
tear worms out of their hair,
then, stiff at first,
so they can hardly move,
their groans soon fill the air.
Articulation slowly returns
and the ghouls begin their dance,
round and round and round they go
lost in a deathly trance.

Don't go to the graveyard on Hallowe'en,
the dead don't like to be found,
they may dance around you,
until they surround you,
then drag you under the ground.

Nigel Gray

Gates

Silently, swiftly, pass this place
where moans like breath of death escape,
where creaks of corkscrewed bones, and cracks
of fingers snapping, taloned taps,
punctuate the shake of chains
as hands of seeking, searching veins
work with the wind to wrestle free
the gates that guard the
                    cemetery.

Gina Douthwaite

Gravestone

I was playing in the churchyard,
When I tripped on a stone –
The name on the gravestone
Was my own!

Sue Cowling

Night Creepers

They prowl the graveyard late at night
and keep their faces out of sight;
they tend to give the bats a fright,

      they want to change their headstones.

They've got no eyes to see the way.
They have to feel their night away.
They never see the light of day,

      they want to change their headstones.

They're so upset they're spitting teeth.
Their rotting flesh smells sickly-sweet.
They have no skin left on their feet,

      they want to change their headstones.

No wooden box could keep them down.
They want pink marble flecked with brown,
require the dearest plaques in town,

      they want to change their headstones.

Barry Woods

Kedge

Tracey Bone – you hurry home
You're late – it's after half-past eight
And in the park when it is dark
Old Kedge the park witch waits

As you pass along the path
Listen for her tread
If you hear it – better fear it
Listen then with dread...

Kedge comes sneaking, softly creeping
Shadow spiky as a tree
Steeple hat and cloak of bats
Her cackles crack with evil glee

Kedge is really weirdly bearded
Sporting warts on every chin
She waits behind the creaking gate
And rides a fitful evening wind

Kedge has twitchy, witchy fingers
Out to clutch your shrinking back
A broom to bear you to her lair
Packed inside a blackened sack –

What will happen when she's got you
Penned inside her dirty den?
Tremble then, for Kedge's victims
Are never *ever* met again!

Better race you silly Tracey
Better run behind the light
Or I betcha Kedge will getcha
As you're going home tonight!

Sally Farrell Odgers

Park Encounter

Shadows in the half-light
Darkening
I shuffle through the park

I hear a fluttering
Whirring
A ghost whispering

An uncertain, shivery sound
Something unseen
Heading my way.

A pale shape
Dives at my face
A blur of wings

I jerk my head away
I stare
At the dark ground

A pale, translucent, moth
On its wings
A black, skull

Death's calling card

Roger Stevens

The Black Dog

The traveller hastens, stumbling down
the lonely road towards the town.
Night has fallen; scared to death,
he hears claws scrape and panting breath.
Clouds hide the moon and all is black.
Small hairs prickle on his back.
'Don't stop, keep moving, don't look round,
behind you pads the ghostly hound
they call Black Shuck; his eyes glow red.
Don't look, for if you look, you're dead.'
The traveller stopped, the traveller turned
and saw great hellfire eyes which burned,
a gleam of fangs, then, empty air.
The black dog was no longer there.
But the traveller trembled in the gloom.
He knew that he was marked for doom.

Marian Swinger

Which Was Which?

It was after
Whatever happened –
Whatever happened?
I can't remember.
But it was after,
And I was walking
Along a street I think that once I must have known.
I was alone.
But then he came towards me,
A young boy,
Intent upon the bouncing of a ball.
Nearer he came, and nearer,
Bounce and skip,
And then he passed right through me
And I turned,
And watched him bouncing, skipping up the road
And did not know
I was the ghost, the ghost who passed through him,
But thought
He was the ghost, a ghost who passed through me.
And I was most afraid.

Pam Gidney

So Dark

It was so dark
  I couldn't see my hand
In front of my face.
  I thought
How do I know it's there?
Maybe there's just air
  Where my hand should be.
So I put my hand up
In the dark
To touch my face
Raised my hand to the place
It should be

And it wasn't there.

Trevor Millum

Turn Back

When dogs start to cower and howl at the moon
and trees fill with faces escaped from cracked tombs

turn back, turn back,

when barns on the bend seem to shelter within
shy shadows, silk see-through, yet shiny as skin

and coaches and horses rasp leaves in their breeze
along the old toll road closed last century

turn back, turn back,

when trees on the hilltop with branches askew
stand outlined like gallows with noose hanging loose

and bonfire embers grow red-eyed with rage
and ash takes the shape of a freshly filled grave

turn back, turn back,

when streams stir up evil in cold cauldron pools

and babble their curses like gossiping ghouls

and wind wraps its fingers in spirals of ice

and sanity's shattered to shards, take advice...

turn back!

Gina Douthwaite

Playing Dead Man's Dip

Put your hand in the bag
And what do you feel?
A dead man's eye
Or a grape that's peeled?

There in the corner,
Some wobbly jelly?
Or the insides
Of a dead man's belly?

A jawful of teeth
All knobbly and hard?
Or mum's old beads
Stuck down on some card?

Rubber bands, perished
And tied up in knots?
Or a dead man's muscles
Beginning to rot?

A soft, squelchy heart
Like a chewed up sphere?
Or the ball you lost
In the garden last year?

What's that you're trying
So hard to grip?
Is it large?
Is it small?
Is it lumpy
Or slimy?
That red on your hand,
What on earth can it be?
Don't ask me!

Patricia Leighton

I Know What It Was

They said it was just
an owl in the tree
but they didn't
fool me!

I saw teeth
not a beak,
red eyes
not gold,
and I won't be told
it was only
a fluff of feathers
round its throat;
it was a collar
and those weren't wings
but the silky folds
of a black, black cloak.

That was no
Too-wit, too-woo
I heard.
It was
I'll get yoo-ou!

Patricia Leighton

MIDNIGHT PROWLERS

Beware!

Midnight chimes and a chill in the air,
It's the witching hour,
Beware!

One o'clock and time for a scare
As ghosts go out haunting,
Beware!

Two o'clock and baleful eyes glare
From the ghouls in the graveyard,
Beware!

Three o'clock and better take care,
The vampires are flying,
Beware!

Four o'clock and a cry of despair
As the werewolves start howling,
Beware!

Five o'clock and lifeless eyes stare
From the corpse-like zombies,
Beware!

And all night long in the icy air
Nightmares come prowling,
Beware!

Cynthia Rider

Midnight Prowler

Castle dweller
Coffin sleeper
Night lover
Midnight prowler
Bat befriender
Cloaked figure
Neck nibbler
Blood sucker

Roger Stevens

Vampires

She gave a slight shudder,
then fell with a thud,
her collar quite suddenly
sodden with blood.

It formed a small puddle.
We fed there, then fled.
And where we had huddled
our victim lay dead.

Nick Toczek

Terror

He wanders through the empty years
conjuring the darkest fears,
red eyed, withered, ashy pale,
a dried leaf harried by the gale
all friends, relations, gone to dust.
They rest in peace. Not he, he must
go on, filled with a grim desire.
Unquenchable, it burns like fire.
Long dead, but still he walks the night.
Sanguineous, his appetite
which craves the life force, hot and red.
He hunts by night, and fully fed
sleeps closeted from lethal light
enclosed by wood and out of sight.
Forests ring his castle walls
and his very name appals.

Marian Swinger

Awakening

Spinning round the vampire's grave,
three witches chant the waking spell,
while monsters prowl within the cave
that holds the gateway into hell.

Now from the earth three demons rise
to open up the vampire mound
and tear the stakes from heart and eyes
that pin her captive in the ground.

Once more this mistress of the night
is free to wander where she will,
to undertake her silent flight
and from your body drink her fill.

She does not live, she cannot die,
you must not gaze upon her face
or with her wishes you'll comply
and serve her in her resting place.

Be watchful now that she is free
for she is seeking you — and me.

Brian G. D'Arcy

A Vampire Valentine

To my Vampire Valentine
May your scary love be mine.
If you shun me, oh what grief!
Please gnaw me with your pointy teeth.

Do not stop, no do not check,
Just bite and bite my thirsty neck.
Your sharp incisors severing skin
Just send me reeling, in a spin.

Oh my sweet Vampire Valentine,
Do not delay, be mine, be mine!

Mike Lack

The Friendly Vampire

'Come in,' the friendly vampire said.
'There's room in my tomb for two.
Together we'll have a late-night bite
And I'll share my drink with you!'

The man shook his head.
'I'd rather be dead!'
The vampire gave a grin.
He took a peck
At the poor man's neck
And greedily sucked him in.

John Foster

To Drac (the Count)

To Drac (the Count)
Director
The Blood Bank
Arterial Road
Gore
Suffolk

Dear Sir,

I wonder if I might enquire
about the job you lately advertised.
It's the position at the blood bank that I'm after.
My C.V. is enclosed. You'd be surprised
at the countless years I've spent just studying
  blood types,
centuries in fact. The rare bouquet
of the fragrant and delicious rhesus negative
excites me as does good old blood type A.
Type B, I always say, has nutty flavour
and type O's the one I favour for dessert

and I can extract the precious fluid by the gallon
with an old technique which really doesn't hurt.
As for pay, don't give me cash, just give me blood
  please
in bags or better still, matured, in vats.

Yours hopefully,
      your most obedient servant,
            Count Vladimir Gracowsky,
                  Vampire Bat.

P.S. By the way, old chap, weren't we at school
  together,
Middle Ages, Transylvania High?
I'll bring a couple of nice fresh peasants with me
and we'll share a jugular or two. Goodbye.

Marian Swinger

33

The Werewolf's Howl

There's a hideous,
horrible, harrowing howl
and you know that a werewolf's
out on the prowl.
So stoke up the fire,
draw curtains tight,
lock all the doors
and keep out the night.
Don't give the werewolf
a chance to get in
for he's thirsty for blood
and hungry for
        skin.

The werewolf's a man
with fingernail claws,
hair on his hands
and slavering jaws.
In anguish and pain
he rages and roars.
He's a werewolf at large
    in the dark
        in the dark.

The werewolf's a man
with red bloodshot eyes
who bays at the moon
in thunderclap skies.

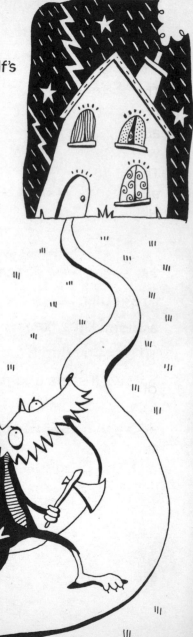

His sharply fanged teeth
can deeply incise.
He's a werewolf at large
    in the dark
        in the dark.

The werewolf's a man
who's seeking a feast,
and only warm flesh
will appease the wild beast.
Those caught in his grip
all end up deceased.
He's a werewolf at large
    in the dark
        in the dark.

There's a hideous,
horrible, harrowing howl
and you know that a werewolf's
out on the prowl.
So stoke up the fire,
draw curtains tight,
lock all the doors
and keep out the night.
Don't give the werewolf
a chance to get in
for he's thirsty for blood
and hungry for
      skin.

Wes Magee

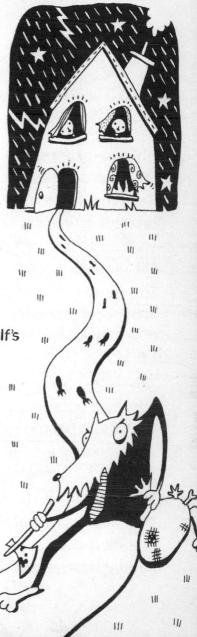

35

The Grey Wolf

In the dark wood
in a clearing
Sleeps a grey wolf
Dreaming, dreaming

His skin is furless
His paws are clawless
He walks into the city
Lawless, lawless

The moon is hidden
The clouds are weeping
A princess slumbers
Sleeping, sleeping

The thief creeps through
The royal bedroom
And steels her ruby
A priceless heirloom

The ruby glows
With fire and lightning
A spell is cast
So frightening, frightening

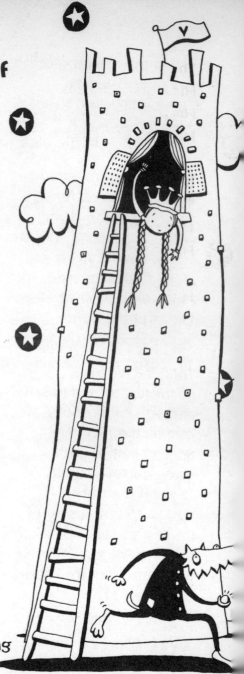

36

The thief grows fur
His body thickens
His hands grow claws
He sickens, sickens

Beneath the black sky
Thunder rumbles
Into the dark wood
He stumbles, stumbles

For in the ruby,
Gleaming, gleaming
A wizard's mind
Is scheming, scheming

Now, in the dark wood
In a clearing
Sleeps a grey wolf
Dreaming, dreaming

Roger Stevens

R.I.P.

R.I.P.
Here resteth
Werewolf
Walter Witz
who chewed relations
into bits.
Aunties, uncles, nephews,
nieces,
all ended up

Ripped In Pieces.

Wes Magee

WANTED - ONE FAMILIAR,
a job for life

Due to an unfortunate accident with a sharpened knife
A vacancy has arisen at the Shady Nook
Home for the elderly. The lucky applicant will work
  directly with the Cook.
We welcome candidates who are not allergic to cats
And have reached at least level six in the B.A.A.T.s*
Double time for any daylight hours worked.
And appropriate penalties for any duties shirked
  (see above).
Feeding matter is on hand throughout the night
Should anybody fancy a quick bite.
If you can do this without breaking a camera,
  Please send a photograph
We won't necessarily choose the vilest, but we
  like to have a laugh.

The Shady Nook Corporation is an evil opportunities
  employer.

*Black Arts Attainment Tests

Petonelle Archer

Thank You, Fangs!

The vampires that bite necks in gangs,
Like a blood which is tasty and tangs,
When they've guzzled enough
Of the hot, pulsing stuff,
They say to their teeth: 'Thank you, fangs!'

Tim Hopkins

We're Werewolves

We're werewolves! We're werewolves!
We howl at the moon.
We're werewolves! We're werewolves!
We're hairy and scary.
Our jaws are like steel traps.
Our claws are like knives.
We're werewolves! We're werewolves!
Be wary! Be wary!

John Foster

FRIGHTENING PHANTOMS AND GHASTLY GHOULS

The Fear

I am the footsteps that crackle on gravel
and the sudden chill that's hard to explain.
I am the figure seen flitting through doorways
and the noisy rattle of a loose window pane.

I am the scream that wakes you at night
with the thought, was it real or a dream?
I am the quickening thud of your heart
and the feeling things aren't what they seem.

I am the slam of a door blown shut
when there isn't even a breeze
and the total and absolute clarity
that you just heard someone sneeze.

I am the midnight visitor,
the knock when there's no one there.
I am the ceiling creaking
and the soft footfall on your stair.

I am the shadows that dance on your wall
and the phantoms that float through your head,
and I am the fear that you fear each night
as you wriggle down deep in your bed.

Brian Moses

The Frightening Phantom

Deep in the Forest of Fear
The Frightening Phantom waits
To pounce on Careless Children
Who stray Beyond the Gates.

Through the Forest of Fear
The Frightening Phantom glides.
In the Dark and Gloomy Glen
The Frightening Phantom hides.

In the Heart of the Forest of Fear
The Frightening Phantom lurks.
The Frightening Phantom snatches.
The Frightening Phantom smirks.

Beware the Frightening Phantom
Which lives in the Forest of Fear.
Take heed of the Witch's Warning:
DON'T GO NEAR!

John Foster

Spooked

When your house feels strange
but you can't say why,
when you wake at night
to the echo of a cry.

When the floorboards creak
to the faintest footfall
and the temperature drops
for no reason at all.

When the rocking chair rocks
but there's no one there,
when something has triggered
your squeaky stair.

When the curtains move
but there isn't a breeze,
when the house is empty
but you hear a sneeze...

You've been spooked
        by a spook,
now you're host
        to a ghost...

Brian Moses

Exploring the Deserted Mansion

In the hall...
cobwebs hang from the crumbling ceiling,
antlered hatstand's carved from oak,
crimson carpet's tattered and torn,
and dust in the air makes you choke.
>Chilly,
>icy mansion.
>Dank,
>deserted place.

In the kitchen...
tarnished taps drip brackish water,
stale loaf's grown a coat of mould,
a foul stench seeps up from the drains,
and the radiators feel stone-cold.
>Fusty,
>fetid mansion.
>Damp,
>deserted place.

On the landing...
a headless, rusty suit of armour,
ancient portrait's green eyes glare,
cracked mirror in a silver frame,
and rat bones on a rocking chair.
>Echoing,
>creaky mansion.
>Dark,
>deserted place.

In the bedroom...
a tousled bed with blood-stained pillow,
rent drapes shiver in the breeze,
cockroach scuttles over floorboards,
and a sudden shriek makes you freeze.
Faded,
pallid mansion.
Dim,
deserted place.

Up in the attic...
frayed dressing gowns have nests of mice,
there's Santa's sack for Christmas Eve,
a vampire bat hangs from a beam,
and the trapdoor's jammed when you try to leave...
Creepy,
scary mansion.
Dead,
deserted place.

Wes Magee

47

The House of Windows

In the house of windows
The curtains are always drawn,
And the faces of the people inside
Pale and thin.

They never see the light anymore,
Only each other's eyes –
Still not realising
They are only each other disguised.

The mirrors in the house of windows
Reflect a pale sick light,
And the one man who lives there
Peers into them each night,

Telling himself he is not alone,
That his friends are with him still –
But all his friends are reflections
of himself sitting old and ill:

And even the man's an illusion
Of shadows and light without breath –
Mirrored and mirrored from room to room
Since the time of his death.

David Greygoose

The Haunted House

Soft footfalls pad across the floor
in the haunted house. Outside your door
are fleshless fingers, scratching, tapping,
bony knuckles, banging, rapping.
Outside the door, deep, hollow groans
mask the sound of jangling bones
and chains which drag and boards that creak
as the door swings open with a squeak
and with staring eyes, you're running, screaming
then sit up suddenly; you're dreaming
in a haunted house. But outside your door,
soft footfalls pad across the floor...

Marian Swinger

Locks

They
lock you in
so without a doubt,
take great care or
you'll never get out!
Some locks have a mind of
their own it seems, and it
makes no difference how much
you scream. The key turns
in the lock with a rusty
creak, and it does
no good
to shout
and
shriek!
So if you
find a door
that swings open
wide, don't be tempted
to step inside, for should you
go over the threshold and past
the jamb, that heavy old door will
suddenly slam, and no matter how much
you scream and shout, once you go in
YOU   CAN   NEVER   GET   OUT   !!

Anne Logan

Where Nobody Lives

I live in the house
where nobody lives

Where the doors never open
where nobody speaks

I live in the house
in the long empty street

Where windows hang open
and broken stairs creak

I live in the house
where the dream children play

We dance through the rooms
till the moon rides away

And I sit by myself
through the slow waiting day

When no-one comes here
and nobody speaks

In the house in the street
where nobody lives

Dave Ward

Fingers

They'd spent a very merry evening
at the old coaching inn
and he agreed, in a mad moment,
to spend the night in the bedroom
they said was haunted.
He was warned about what had
happened there: unexplained things
that had left anyone who slept there
shaken, silent, changed.
All rot, he said, superstitious rubbish.

. . . . .

Alone in the room later, with bravery
leaking away, he makes the best of it.
Searches the room... nowhere to hide...
No one. None too clean: a few earwigs
but the bed's fine. Door locked;
bolted too on the inside.
Window fastened. And so to bed,
matches handy on the bedside table
just in case. Puff out the candle
and now head down till morning.

. . . . .

From deep sleep he comes wide awake,
completely alert in an instant.
Pitch black. The only sounds
his own breath and heart.
What woke him? His flesh crawls
with a sense of strangeness.
He knows he is not alone.
Light the candle. Matches...
He feels for them... sweeps the table
with his hand.
Gone.
And then the fingers brush his hand,
cold fingers stop his searching hand
and give him the matchbox.

Eric Finney

The Haunted Castle

Here I walk and here I dream,

dust motes twinkling in a beam

of sunlight shafting through the gloom.

Above me, great stone towers loom

Till these dark towers fall, I wait

through endless years, it is my fate

to drift unseen, unloved, long dead.

Carrying my severed head,

I pace this mighty castle keep

and as I pace, I sometimes weep.

Then people shiver and they say,

'The ghost! The ghost has passed this way.'

Marian Swinger

Mirror

I gaze into the mirror
On the dusty, crumbling wall
In the gloomy room
At the ghostly end
Of the ancient castle wall.
And what do I see
In the silvered glass?

No sign of me at all!

John Kitching

The Fiend Fair of Horror

Don't miss the great Fiend Fair of Horror;
experience the frights and the freaks.
Try the mind blowing rides
which melt your insides
and put you on bed rest for weeks.

Go on the ghost train; real phantoms
will fix bony hands round your neck.
Don't bother to shriek,
you'll be there for a week
and come out a gibbering wreck.

Then jump on the fearful big dipper
which travels much faster than sound
and go to your doom
with a huge sonic boom
as you hurtle, mind gone, to the ground.

Try our freak show; the freaks are real demons
whose features will turn you to stone
or visit Great Jing,
the cannibal king
who'll reduce you to nothing but bones.

There's the sinister chamber of mirrors
distorting all sizes and shapes.
One party who gazed
were aggrieved and amazed
to emerge as a party of apes.

The coconut shy is quite novel
as for coconuts we use real heads,
so give it a shot,
winner or not,
you can take one away; they're quite dead.

So please come to the fiend fair of Horror,
yes, flow through our portals in shoals.
It's really quite funny,
we don't want your money;
the entry fee's merely your souls.

Marian Swinger

In a Dungeon

Now I stand alone in the dungeon,
Feel the chill of its bare earth floor
And I seem to hear across centuries
The slam of its great oak door;
The chink of chains, the scuttle of rats
And the groans of men in despair.
The stories these mossy walls might tell
Hang in the cold, damp air.
This is a place of misery
And hopelessness and fear.
Now the only thought in my mind is:
Let me get out of here!

Eric Finney

CHILLING CREATURES AND PERILOUS PLACES

The Creeper

One look at the Creeper
Will fill you with awe
His mouth is a cavern
A vice is his jaw.

His girth is prodigious
The kind you acquire
When appetite burns
Like a forest on fire.

His teeth are an arsenal
Of blades and machetes
With power enough
For dismembering Yetis.

His gut is a cess pool
Of juices corrosive
And poisonous acid
And gases explosive.

His throat like a drainpipe
Will carry you down
In a river of mucous
You'll struggle, then drown.

His bowel a dungeon
A pit of despair
And all those who enter
Will perish in there.

He'll lure you with cunning
Beguile you with lies
But whatever you do
Don't look into his eyes.

They are swollen with evil
Distended with malice
His motives are wicked
His methods are callous.

For this is the Creeper
He'll fill you with awe
His mouth is a cavern
A vice is his jaw.

Granville Lawson

Hoblins and Boglins

Hoblins and Boglins are evil and mean,
Rotten and troublesome, ugly, obscene,
Horrid and horrible, manic and green
Planting their nightmares into your dream

Hoblins and Boglins are poison and spite
Shouting out lies in your ears late at night
Making up monsters and creatures that bite
Anything nasty to give you a fright

Hoblins and Boglins have souls deepest black
Choosing the darkest of night to attack
But when the sun shines and dawn starts to crack
They shrivel away and never come back...

Until midnight strikes and daylight has gone
The Hoblins and Boglins are creeping out from
The shadows of shadows to wreak havoc on
The innocent daughter and carefree young son

teeth

For Hoblins and Boglins are evil and mean
Rotten and troublesome, ugly, obscene,
Horrid and horrible, manic and green
They muffle your mouth and silence your scream

Yes Hoblins and Boglins are poison and spite
Embracing the wrong and loathing the right
Hating the daytime, loving the night,
They breathe in the dark but choke in the light.

Paul Cookson

Why Are We Hiding In Here?

Why are we hiding in here?
Why are we hiding in here?
What's up? What's there? What makes you stare?
Why are we hiding in here?

Why are we hiding in here?
Is it that breathing noise coming near?
Is that the thing I've got to fear?

Why are we hiding in here?
Is it that shape that's begun to appear?
Is that the thing I've got to fear?

Why are we hiding in here?
Is it that outline becoming clear?
Is that the thing I've got to fear?

Don't tell me that there's nothing to fear
I know there's something coming near
And nothing you say will make it disappear
Oh why, oh why are we hiding in here?

Trevor Millum

Who Lies?

Who lies in the deep of the pond
In the park.
Who's whispering under the weeds?
Is it a witch with a wand
In the dark,
Dreaming of spells that she needs?

Who shivers the pond
In the heat of the day?
Who causes the goldfish to hide?
Who causes the heron
To leap into flight
And leave little children wide-eyed?

Is it a witch
On a watery ride
Or something more wicked
That's deep inside
That dark
Of the pond in the park?

John Kitching

KEEP OUT!

Hungry

From the dark primeval depths
of the lake that workmen dredge,

something slippery slithers
to the surface, to the edge,

some strange freak of evolution
oozing over the reeds and sedge.

Something sluggish slides tonight
smoothly through the moonless hedge.

Something sticky, thick and viscous
sludges past the blooms and veg.

Something slimy's slowly climbing
onto the open window-ledge...

Nick Toczek

Oh! The Hole

Oh! The Hole is deep and dark
and Oh! The Hole is dense.
Full of rotting forests, swamps
and sounds to turn you tense.
It smells of burnt potatoes
and sewers sickly ripe.
A swirling and a scheming place
for every dangerous type.

Oh! The Hole is menacing
and Oh! The Hole is wide.
A blur of mist and mildew fogs
and clouds of cyanide
where sun and bird song can not be
and kindness can not breathe.
Oh! Please be sure you don't fall in
the Hole you'll never leave.

Stewart Henderson

Deep Down In the Darkness

Deep
down
in the darkness
of an octopus ocean,
deep
down
in the squid-ridden,
sharkery sea,
the slime beasts
are mating,
the slime beasts
are waiting
for the end of the world,
and for you,
and for me.

Deep
down
in the mudmurk
of an oyster-squashed ocean,
deep
down
in the skate-smelly
sandsquishy sea,
the slime beasts
aren't sleeping,

the slime beasts
are creeping
to the end of the world,
and for you,
and for me.

Deep
down
in the inkpitch
of an oozeboozy ocean,
deep
down
in the seaweedy,
shipwreck-strewn sea,
the slime beasts
are slumming,
the slime beasts
are coming...

it's the end of the world,
and for you,
and for

me.

Wes Magee

69

Leviathan

There are salt sea tales
Of great white whales
And monsters of the Deep,
Of the red-eyed shark
Which swims in the dark
And never ever sleeps
There are octopuses
The size of buses
And a clam with a giant jaw
Gargantuan rays
Which spend their days
On the ocean's sandy floor.

There are mariners' yarns
Of fish with arms
And squids that can squeeze you to death,
Of Mermaids fair
With seaweed hair
That can turn you to stone with their breath,

There are fire-breathing eels
And two headed seals
And a crab with a giant claw
Pale creatures of jelly
That lay on their belly
On the ocean's sandy floor.

But such legends of old
Don't compare with those told
Of the greatest sea monster of all.
Its long deadly tail
Is covered in scales
And its head is a fiery ball.
The teeth sharp and white
Have a venomous bite
And it utters a deafening roar.
The huge eyes they glow
As it drags you below
To the ocean's sandy floor.

Gervase Phinn

Cave

Rumpled rock faces
with green seaweed hair
suck air and grumble.

Beware child, beware.

Cold skittled echoes roll round the wet walls,
cracks in the roof dribble green waterfalls,

waves bite at toes sinking spiked teeth of ice,
seas seize at knees freezing blood in a vice,

gulls fly past screaming with wild, warning calls
there in the darkness where no sunshine falls

rumpled rock faces
with green seaweed hair
suck air and grumble.

Beware child, beware.

Gina Douthwaite

Caves

Caves are hungry,

caves are hollow,

caves with children in them

swallow.

Gina Douthwaite

Grey Landscape

There are rocks on every side
that seem to creep and lunge,
but they're strangely soft to touch
like a soapy soggy sponge,
and the grey ground under my feet
seems to rock and roll
      and rise and plunge.

There's a sound like the hum of a wire
and from time to time there's a spark,
crossing my path as I stumble along,
like a lightning flash in the dark,
and a regular pulse throbs all around
like the boom of a drum in a jungle,
      or the beat of a thumping heart.

I have reached a wall of white
that feels as hard as stone,
encasing the grisly hills
in a curving sky of bone.
Although I knock and kick and cry
I find no answer, and nobody comes:
      I'm all alone.

I feel as if I am drowning
in a terrible cerebral sea,
where someone is thinking so hard,
their thoughts are swallowing me.
I'm sinking fast in a brainwave
locked up in the skull of a giant;
and I as small as a flea.

Celia Warren

Banshee

Bar the door
And bolt the shutter!
No-one stir,
Speak or mutter.
Hark! Can you hear it,
Eerily howling,
Endlessly prowling?

Gervase Phinn

SINISTER SHADOWS
AND
NIGHTMARE
SCREAMS

What's That?

What's that scratching
at the window pane?
Who's that knocking
again and again?
What's that creeping
across the floor?
And who's that tapping
at my bedroom door?

What's that creaking
beneath my bed?
Who's that walking
with slow slow tread?
What's whirr whirring
in the air?
And who's that coming
up the squeaky stair?

Wes Magee

Shadows

Sinister shadows stretch, creeping
over the ceiling at night.
Hideous shapes in the moonlight
loom on the edges of sight.
Flickering figures flit faster,
nightmare shapes creep up the wall
but you know they're just stupid old shadows
and shadows can't hurt you at all.
So you snuggle down under your duvet
and slip into mild, pleasant dreams
and the shadows close in, red eyes glowing
and nobody hears as you scream.

Marian Swinger

We Are Not Alone

When floorboards creak and hinges squeak
When the TV's off but seems to speak
When the moon is full and you hear a shriek
We are not alone.

When the spiders gather beneath your bed
When they colonise the garden shed
When they spin their webs right above your head
We are not alone.

When the lights are out and there's no-one home
When you're by yourself and you're on your own
When the radiators bubble and groan
We are not alone.

When the shadows lengthen round your wall
When you hear deep breathing in the hall
When you think there's no-one there at all
We are not alone.

When the branches tap on your window pane
When finger twigs scritch scratch again
When something's changed but it looks the same
We are not alone.

When the wallpaper is full of eyes
When the toys in the dark all change in size
When anything's a monster in disguise
We are not alone.

You'd better watch out whatever you do
There's something out there looking at you
When you think you are on your own
We are not
We are not
We are not alone.

Paul Cookson

81

Beware! Beware!

It's coming.
    It's creeping.
        It's watching, it's waiting,
    it's waiting, it's watching.
It's creeping,
    It's coming.

    Beware!
        Beware!

There's something there.
        watching from its secret lair.

Waiting for the dead of night,
        waiting till you're tucked in tight.

Watching with its icy stare,
        knowing you are unaware.

Coming to give you a fright,
        creeping slowly, out of sight.

Knowing you are lying there,
        it's coming.

It's coming,
  it's coming,
    it's coming,
      it's coming,
        it's coming,

  so   Beware!
      shhh!   Beware!

Brian G. D'Arcy

Bathroom Bug

It lives in the bathroom,
it slides on the floor,
it hides in dark corners
where dust makes it snore.

It's hairy and spiky
and sticky with goo.
When you're in the bathroom
it's looking at you.

Gina Douthwaite

Nightmare

I locked the door;
The cat I fed;
I climbed the stairs
To go to bed.
But then I froze
With troubled stare
To find myself
Already there...

Trevor Harvey

Nightmare

Screech of owl
In the gloom of night,
Phantom shapes
And vampire's bite,
Warlock's curse
And werewolf's howl,
Gaping tombs
And banshee howl,
Lurching zombies
And sightless stares,
A seething cauldron
Of nightmare scares.

Cynthia Rider

Nameless Fears

They ride on the wings of the darkest night
And they roam across the land,
Clawing at windows and scratching at doors
With their bloodless, bony hands.

They creep furtively into your nightmares
Whispering of darkness and death,
You have felt the clammy touch of their skin
And the icy chill of their breath.

You have glimpsed them in sighing shadows
Like a fleeting trick of the light,
And you know there is no escape from the grip
Of the nameless fears of the night!

Cynthia Rider

Night Night

Night night, sleep tight,

Don't let the bedbugs bite.

They'll burrow underneath your skin

And eat you from the outside in

Until you're just a skeleton

And even that will soon be gone.

Then everything that once was you

Will end up sticky, slimy goo.

Night night, sleep tight,

Don't let the bedbugs bite.

Marcus Parry

Blood and Bones

Under the floorboards, cold and deep,
Pipes are laid that drip and seep.
Down below the house, in the damp, dark mud,
Do they drip water or do they drip...?

Blood in my arteries!
Blood in my veins!
I dreamt that blood ran
down the drains!

High above the ceilings rafters creak.
Blind bats blunder. Mad mice squeak.
Up in the roof there are rattles and moans.
Is it the wind or chains and...?

Bones in my body!
Bones in my head!
I dreamt there was a skeleton
in my bed!

Celia Warren

A Strangler's Hand

It's happening now, as it did once before,
  but this time, it's come to settle some score.
The simple fact is, that what opened the door
  is a grave-spotted hand, and not a thing more.

No arm, and no body — just a leathery hand
  that comes groping towards me where I stand,
with the air freezing all around it, and
  the fear of it fills my mouth like dry sand.

I'd feel a bit easier if only it grew
  from the arm and the body of... no matter who!
And my terror might slacken, if only I knew
  what it is the grim horror is trying to do.

Now it's inches away, and it just seems to float,
  and it's flexing its fingers to come at my throat,
but rather than strike, it just hangs there to gloat,
  while I cringe rabbit-like from the pounce of a stoat!

Raymond Wilson

Nightmare

You go to bed
You fall asleep
And then your flesh
Begins to creep.

A pack of wolves
Is chasing you
They want your
Arms and legs to chew.

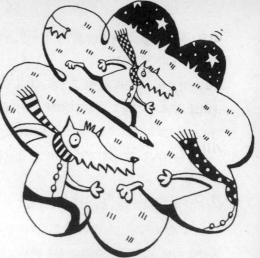

You try to run
But down below
Your legs and feet
Refuse to go.

They're catching you
They're catching you
They want your
Arms and legs to chew.

They're closing in
They're closing in
You feel their breath
Upon your skin.

Surrounding you
Surrounding you
They want your
Arms and legs to chew.

Will you become
A tasty snack
Or dog meat for
This evil pack?

They're threatening you
They're threatening you
They want your
Arms and legs to chew.

Is this the end?
You start to scream
You can't escape
This nightmare dream.

Granville Lawson

The Ghostly Executioner

Clomping footsteps on the stairs
Feel the fear prickling your hairs.
Clomp, Clomp. Then the door creaks.
A deathly silence – no one speaks.
Before you the Ghostly Executioner stands,
A bloodied axe in his bloodied hands.
He died in mid-chop. He dropped like a stone.
His poor victim's half-severed head gave a groan.
He can't rest till he's hacked off another head,
And he's marching, marching towards your bed.
As he raises the axe you hear yourself scream
And you wake drenched in sweat from your nightmare dream.

Tim Pointon

I Thought It Was Just a Nightmare

I thought it was just a nightmare,
that it happened in my sleep
but this morning on my pillow
I found some things to keep...

A silver cross, a snakeskin,
A golden eagle's claw,
One twisted finger, broken,
One footprint on the floor.

I thought it was just a nightmare
but that's not how it seems
for the things I found this morning
I first saw in my dreams.

Paul Cookson

Get You

He drew a monster
on the inside cover
of his library book.
That was at bedtime,
but he fell asleep.

By morning
his monster
seemed bigger,
its eyes
more open wide,
its ears more pointed.
A drop of blood
flecked its chin.

By bedtime
that night
it was inching
towards the edge of the paper.
As he quickly closed the book
the monster grinned.

Brian Morse

Acknowledgements

We are grateful to the following authors for permission to include the following poems, all of which are published for the first time in this collection:

Petonelle Archer: 'WANTED – ONE FAMILIAR, a Job For Life' copyright © Petonelle Archer 2003. Ian Bland: 'Will You Come Down To The Graveyard?' copyright © Ian Bland 2003. Paul Cookson: 'Hoblins and Boglins' and 'I Thought It Was Just a Nightmare' both copyright © Paul Cookson 2003. Sue Cowling: 'Gravestone' copyright © Sue Cowling 2003. Brian G. D'Arcy: 'Awakening' and 'Beware! Beware!' both copyright © Brian G. D'Arcy 2003. Gina Douthwaite: 'Turn Back', 'Cave' and 'Caves' all copyright © Gina Douthwaite 2003. Eric Finney: 'Fingers' and 'In a Dungeon' both copyright © Eric Finney 2003. John Foster: 'We're Werewolves!' and 'The Frightening Phantom' both copyright © John Foster 2003. Pam Gidney: 'Which Was Which?' copyright © Pam Gidney 2003. Nigel Gray: 'The Dance' copyright © Nigel Gray 2003. David Greygoose: 'The House of Windows' copyright © David Greygoose 2003. Trevor Harvey: 'Nightmare' copyright © Trevor Harvey 2003. Stewart Henderson: 'Oh! The Hole' copyright © Stewart Henderson 2003. John Kitching: 'Mirror' and 'Who Lies?' both copyright © John Kitching 2003. Mike Lack: 'A Vampire Valentine' copyright © Mike Lack 2003. Granville Lawson: 'The Creeper' and 'Nightmare' both copyright © Granville Lawson 2003. Anne Logan: 'Locks' copyright © Anne Logan 2003. Patricia Leighton: 'I Know What It Was' and 'Playing Dead Man's Dip' both copyright © Patricia Leighton 2003. Wes Magee: 'The Werewolf's Howl', 'R.I.P.', 'Exploring the Deserted Mansion', 'What's That?' and 'Deep Down In the Darkness' all copyright © Wes Magee 2003. Trevor Millum: 'So Dark' and 'Why Are We Hiding In Here?' both copyright © Trevor Millum 2003. Brian Moses: 'The Fear' and 'Spooked' both copyright © Brian Moses 2003. Marcus Parry: 'Night Night' copyright © Marcus Parry 2003. Gervase Phinn: 'Banshee' and 'Leviathan' both copyright © Gervase Phinn 2003. Tim Pointon: 'The Ghostly Executioner' copyright © Tim Pointon 2003. Cynthia Rider: 'Beware!', 'Nightmare' and 'Nameless Fears' all copyright © Cynthia Rider 2003. Roger Stevens: 'Park Encounter', 'Midnight Prowler' and 'The Grey Wolf' all copyright © Roger Stevens 2003. Marian Swinger: 'The Black Dog', 'Terror', 'To Drac (the Count)', 'The Haunted House', 'The Haunted Castle', 'The Fiend Fair of Horror' and 'Shadows' all copyright © Marian Swinger 2003. Nick Toczek: 'Vampires' and 'Hungry' both copyright © Nick Toczek 2003. Dave Ward: 'Where Nobody Lives' copyright © Dave Ward

2003. Celia Warren: 'Grey Landscape' copyright © Celia Warren 2003. Barry Woods: 'Night Creepers' copyright © Barry Woods 2003.

We also acknowledge permission to include previously published poems:

Paul Bright: 'Sinister Symphony' copyright © Paul Bright 2002, first published in *Shorts* compiled by Paul Cookson (Macmillan Children's Books), included by permission of the author. Paul Cookson 'We Are Not Alone' copyright © 1999 Paul Cookson, first published in *We Are Not Alone* (Macmillan), included by permission of the author. Gina Douthwaite: 'Gates' copyright © 1999 Gina Douthwaite, first published in *We Are Not Alone* compiled by Paul Cookson (Macmillan Children's Books) and 'Bathroom Bug' copyright © 2000 Gina Douthwaite, first published in *Spectacular Spooks*, compiled by Brian Moses (Macmillan Children's Books), both included by permission of the author. John Foster: 'The Friendly Vampire' copyright © 2001 John Foster, first published in *Word Wizard* (Oxford University Press), included by permission of the author. Tim Hopkins: 'Thank You, Fangs!' copyright © Tim Hopkins, included by permission of the author. Brian Morse: 'Get You' copyright © 1994 Brian Morse from *Plenty of Time* (Bodley Head), included by permission of the author. Sally Farrell Odgers: 'Kedge' copyright © 1986 Sally Farrell Odgers, included by permission of the author. Celia Warren: 'Blood and Bones' copyright © Celia Warren 1994, first published in *Dracula's Auntie Ruthless* compiled by David Orme (Macmillan Children's Books), included by permission of the author. Raymond Wilson: 'A Strangler's Hand' copyright © 1991 Raymond Wilson, included by permission of Mrs G. Wilson.